Josie's Troubles

Books by Phyllis Reynolds Naylor

Witch's Sister
Witch Water
The Witch Herself
Walking through the Dark
How I Came to Be a Writer
How Lazy Can You Get?
Eddie, Incorporated
All Because I'm Older
Shadows on the Wall
Faces in the Water
Footprints at the Window
The Boy with the Helium Head
A String of Chances
The Solomon System
The Mad Gasser of Bessledorf Street
Night Cry
Old Sadie and the Christmas Bear
The Dark of the Tunnel
The Agony of Alice
The Keeper
The Bodies in the Bessledorf Hotel
The Year of the Gopher
Beetles, Lightly Toasted
Maudie in the Middle
One of the Third Grade Thonkers
Alice in Rapture, Sort Of
Keeping a Christmas Secret
Bernie and the Bessledorf Ghost
Send No Blessings
Reluctantly Alice
Shiloh
King of the Playground
Josie's Troubles

PHYLLIS REYNOLDS NAYLOR

ILLUSTRATIONS BY SHELLEY MATHEIS

ATHENEUM · 1992 · NEW YORK
Maxwell Macmillan Canada
TORONTO
Maxwell Macmillan International
NEW YORK OXFORD SINGAPORE SYDNEY

Atheneum
Macmillan Publishing Company
866 Third Avenue
New York, NY 10022

Maxwell Macmillan Canada, Inc.
1200 Eglinton Avenue East
Suite 200
Don Mills, Ontario M3C 3N1
Macmillan Publishing Company is part of the Maxwell Communication Group of Companies.

Printed in the United States of America

2 3 4 5 6 7 8 9 10

Book design by Patrice Fodero

LIBRARY OF CONGRESS CATALOGING-IN-PUBLICATION DATA

Naylor, Phyllis Reynolds.
Josie's troubles/by Phyllis Reynolds Naylor.—1st ed.
p. cm.
Summary: Josie and Sarah, two West Virginia fourth-graders, break one of the legs of Sarah's mother's piano bench, and must take a series of odd jobs in order to raise the money to repair it.
ISBN 0-689-31659-3
[1. Friendship—Fiction.] I. Title.
PZ7.N24Jo 1992
[Fic]—dc20 90-47641

To the memory of
Bethany and Brittany Grinder,
who loved books,
and to their parents, Pamela and Michael,
who passed that love along

Contents

Josie's Troubles

Chapter One

How It All Began

"It's the worst thing we've ever done," said Josephine to her friend, the friend she seemed to have been waiting for all her life.

Sarah nodded miserably. They had just fallen over backward on the piano bench. Sarah sat rubbing her arm, but Josephine was looking at the broken leg of the bench.

She had tried to be helpful. Sarah was having trouble with her piano lessons, and Josephine offered to play the bottom notes while Sarah played the top. They practiced it three times.

After that they had played "Chopsticks," and then Sarah taught Josephine how to play one part of a duet by hitting high C with her fist and rolling her knuckles over the next three notes. When they'd mastered that, they had a stand-up piano race.

Sarah had started at the bottom note of the piano,

MOZART
Con

Josephine started at the top, and they had to play every key, black keys included, as fast as they could to see who got to middle C first. The first one to reach it sat down on the piano bench and won the game.

On the very first race, they both reached middle C about the same time, they both tried to sit down on the piano bench first, and they both went over backward.

"Mom will kill me," said Sarah.

Josephine Wells and her family had moved into the house at the bottom of the hill only six weeks before; already the two girls were best friends, and already they were in trouble.

"Do you have any glue?" Josephine asked.

"Elmer's," said Sarah.

They glued the leg of the piano bench back together, and by the time Mrs. Prescott came home later with Caroline, Sarah's older sister, the piano bench was standing again, the crack in the wooden leg was invisible, and Josephine and Sarah were quietly reading *Ramona Quimby* books on the couch.

Mrs. Prescott took off her jacket. "I'm so happy that you and Sarah are friends," she told Josephine. "It has made such a difference around here since the Stumps moved away and your family moved in."

Josephine smiled her best smile, the kind where her teeth stayed together but her lips came apart and the corners of her mouth stretched halfway to China.

"Thank you," she said.

"Are you beginning to feel at home in Webster Springs?"

"Yes, ma'am," said Josephine.

"And your mother and father like it here too?"

"Yes, ma'am," Josephine said again. She had learned to say "ma'am" back in Summersville. The third grade teacher in Summersville made you say "yes, ma'am" and "no, ma'am" every time you opened your mouth. You said it to anybody who was more than fifteen years old. Josephine got so used to saying it that whenever her mother called, "Josephine Ruth!" instead of "Josie!" Josephine automatically said, "ma'am?"

"Good," said Mrs. Prescott. "I'm glad your parents like Webster Springs."

Josephine skipped back down the hill to her house, glad that they had managed to fix the piano bench. Her biggest fear, when her family left Summersville, was that she would not find a friend in Webster Springs. A real friend, a best friend, a girl who liked you better than anyone else. She had never had a best friend in Summersville, and when she entered fourth grade here in her new town, it seemed that most of the girls in her class already had best friends. Sarah, in fact, had been best friends with Kimberly Evans. But little by little, Sarah seemed to be liking Josie the best.

Perhaps it was because they both had brown eyes

and brown hair, though Josephine's hair was straight and short and Sarah's was straight and long.

Perhaps it was because they both liked to roller-skate, they both loved chocolate-covered grahams, and neither one of them especially liked dolls.

But they were also friends because Josephine's family had moved into the house where a boy used to live who threw walnuts at Sarah's legs on the way to school; Sarah would never have to worry about that again.

When Josephine went inside, she told her parents what Mrs. Prescott had said about being glad that the Wellses had come to Webster Springs.

"That's nice," said Josie's mother. She was dishing up beef and noodles for Vernon, who was eleven, Clyde, who was sixteen, and Josie's father. "It's good to have a special friend, and her a doctor's daughter."

Mother always said that about Sarah, as though being a doctor's daughter made her different somehow. She didn't look any different to Josephine—had the same number of arms and legs as anybody else. Even wore the same kind of underpants.

The Prescotts, in turn, liked Josephine because she was polite. Sarah told her so, and then they both laughed. The Prescotts had never seen Josephine eat spaghetti. She didn't look very polite then.

"Dr. Prescott sure must make a lot of money," said Clyde. "Nice big car like he drives."

"Big fancy house," said Vernon.

"And good-looking daughters?" Josie's father said to Clyde.

"Ugh and double ugh," was all Clyde said, and went on eating noodles.

The minute supper was over, the phone rang. It was Sarah.

"Daddy's madrigal group is coming here tonight and I have to be quiet," she said. "Do you want to come up?"

"What's a madrigal group?" Josephine wanted to know.

"People who sit around and sing old songs. *Real* old songs—back when there were castles, I think."

"What could we do?" Josephine wondered.

"We could watch them from the top of the stairs," Sarah suggested. "They sit there opening and closing their mouths like goldfish."

That sounded like a marvelous way to spend an evening, so Josephine went up the hill to the Prescotts', and she and Sarah sat in the dark at the top of the stairs as the singers began to arrive.

There were tall men and short men and fat women and skinny women. They all sat around in a circle with their backs straight, holding their songbooks out in front of them and—just as Sarah said—opening and closing their mouths like goldfish.

Josephine and Sarah decided to give them each names.

"Goldie," Sarah whispered to Josephine, pointing to a tiny woman with orange hair.

"Sharkie," said Josephine, pointing to a tall man with a long nose.

"Flounder," Sarah named her father, Dr. Prescott, who directed the group, sitting on the very edge of his chair, holding his book with one hand and waving his other in time to the music.

The girls giggled softly.

"No, no!" the Flounder said, stopping the song. "Tenors, you came in too soon again. It's one . . . 'Here' . . . three . . . four . . . 'lies my heart'. . . ."

All the fish tried again, and again one of the tenors did it wrong. More giggles from the top of the stairs.

"No, no, no!" said Dr. Prescott, and this time he went over to the piano, pulled out the bench, sat down to play the notes, and promptly crashed to the floor.

Josephine and Sarah stared in horror.

"What on earth happened?" asked Mrs. Prescott, coming into the room.

The other fish were trying not to laugh, Josephine could tell.

"Search me," said Dr. Prescott, as he got to his feet again, his face as red as his sweater. "All I did was sit down and the piano bench broke."

One of the singers was examining the leg of the bench. "Looks as though it were broken before and someone tried to glue it back together." He sniffed at it. "Elmer's glue," he said.

Josephine and Sarah fled to Sarah's room and shut the door, but a minute later it opened and there stood Sarah's mother.

"What happened?" she asked, her arms folded across her chest.

Shakily, Sarah explained what had happened that afternoon; Josephine stared down at her knees.

"That is a rosewood piano," said Mrs. Prescott, "and I'll never be able to find another bench to match it. I'll have to take the bench to a furniture expert and have the leg repaired or replaced. I don't know how much it will cost, Sarah, but you were responsible, and I expect you to earn the money to pay for it."

She went back out and closed the door.

Josephine felt awful. She knew that Sarah's mother was really scolding her too, and she deserved it.

"Don't worry," she told her friend. "I'll help you earn the money."

And that's when the trouble *really* began.

Chapter Two

Dear Mr. Quarterback

Josephine lay on her bed without moving. She could hear the television in the next room where her father and brothers were watching football. Sometimes Josephine watched too. She'd make a big bowl of popcorn for all of them, and her brothers would explain what was happening in the game.

But tonight she did not want to watch television. She didn't want to eat popcorn. She wasn't sure she would ever be hungry again. She was afraid that, because of what happened, the Prescotts would be angry, and Sarah would start liking Kimberly best again. She tried to figure out how much a new leg for a piano bench would cost. A *rosewood* piano bench, Mrs. Prescott had said, which probably meant that it was very, very expensive.

"Josie?" Mother stood in the doorway. "I *thought* I heard you come in. Why are you lying here in the dark?"

"I'm just resting my eyes."

Mother was quiet a moment. "Weren't you going up to Sarah's?"

"I did, but I came home again," Josephine said. Mother ought to be able to figure that out for herself.

This time Mother was quiet even longer. "You and Sarah didn't have a quarrel, did you?" she asked finally.

"We *never* quarrel," said Josephine. "I just felt like coming home, that's all."

It *wasn't* exactly all, of course, but it was as much as Josephine wanted to tell. Mother went back to the living room again, while Josephine thought about pianos.

If she knew how much a piano cost, she might be able to figure out how much they'd have to pay for a bench. Would a rosewood piano cost a thousand dollars? Fifty thousand dollars? Half a million? She didn't even know how much half a million was, but maybe it wasn't too much for a rosewood piano.

She thought she remembered seeing some pianos advertised in the newspaper the last day or two. So she went out in the kitchen and looked through the stack by the back door.

The paper with the pianos in it was the very last one in the pile. There were pictures of three pianos: one for two thousand dollars, one for five thousand dollars, and one for eleven thousand. The ad didn't say anything at all about a rosewood piano. A rosewood piano—a rosewood *grand* piano, like the

Prescotts'—would probably cost fifteen thousand at least, Josephine decided.

Okay, she thought. If a rosewood piano cost fifteen thousand dollars, how much would only one leg of a rosewood piano bench cost? She tried to think how many legs would equal a whole piano. She imagined herself piling one piano bench leg on top of another, stacks and stacks of piano bench legs, until all the stacks together were as high and as wide as a grand piano. About two hundred, she guessed. Two hundred piano bench legs would equal a whole piano.

She went out in the living room and sat down between her brothers.

"Vernon," she said, when a commercial came on, "if a whole piano costs fifteen thousand dollars, how much would a two-hundredth of a piano cost?"

"That's stupid," said Vernon. "Who would want to buy just a piece of a piano?"

Josephine sat through the next part of the game, and when another commercial came on she asked her older brother. "Clyde," she said, "if a piano costs fifteen thousand dollars, how much would two-hundredths of it cost?"

"That's easy, Josie," Clyde told her. "Figure it out for yourself."

Josephine wasn't so good at arithmetic. "Divide?" she guessed.

Clyde nodded.

Josephine slid off the couch and reached for a pencil on the coffee table. She scribbled some numbers on the side of the newspaper. Her heart sank. She walked to the phone in the hallway.

"Sarah?" she said softly after dialing the Prescotts' number, relieved that Sarah had answered and not her mother. "We're in trouble."

"You're telling me?" said Sarah.

"I think I know how much it would cost to get another leg for the piano bench."

"How much?"

"Seven thousand and five hundred dollars. We'll have to rob a bank."

"Seven thousand five hundred dollars!" Sarah gasped. "How do you know?"

Josephine explained why she divided fifteen thousand dollars and no cents by two hundred dollars, and what she got.

"Wait a minute," said Sarah. She was gone a long time. When she came back she said, "I asked Caroline to do it for us, Josie. You forgot the decimal point. It's only seventy-five."

"Whew!" said Josephine, relieved.

"We're still in trouble," said Sarah. "How do we earn seventy-five dollars? I never had seventy-five dollars in my life! All I've got right now is two dollars."

"We'll think of a way," Josephine told her, then added, "I guess you're lucky it wasn't you and *Kimberly* who sat down on the bench and broke it, because Kimberly's so heavy she'd probably have broken *two* legs!"

Kimberly wasn't all *that* heavy, but she *might* have broken two legs of the bench, Josephine decided as she went back and sat between her brothers on the couch.

"Did you see that pass, Josie?" cried her father. "Wow! The *arm* on that guy! Greg Maloney is the best quarterback in the NFL, and he went to high school right here in West Virginia."

Josie watched the game for a while. "How much money do quarterbacks make?" she wondered.

"Ha!" said Vernon. "Millions!"

"A million, anyway," said Josie's father.

Josephine stared at the quarterback. He probably had a rosewood piano in *his* house. He probably had *three* of them, and even if he didn't, he certainly had seventy-five dollars to spare.

She got a piece of paper, an envelope, and a stamp from the family desk and took them to her room to write a letter:

Dear Mr. Quarterback:

My dad says you are the best quarterback in the country and you have a great arm. He watches all your games. My brothers watch your games too. Vernon says you make a million dollars playing football.

That's why I'm writing to you. I don't need a lot of money, only seventy-five dollars. I knocked over a piano bench and broke one of the legs, and I have to pay for it, and I only have $3.71. My friend has to pay for it too, and she only has two dollars.

If you have some extra money, I would be very happy if you would send some of it to me. I can pay you back if you want. Even if you don't send me any, I will still watch your games. Sometimes.

Josephine Wells

Josephine had no idea where Greg Maloney lived, so she just wrote on the envelope:

Greg Maloney
Best Quarterback in the Country
Football
America

Then she put her own address in the upper left-hand corner and a stamp on the envelope, and walked down to the corner to mail it.

The next morning she went out on the sidewalk and waited for Sarah. They walked to school together every day. If Sarah had cereal for breakfast, she was usually on time. But if she had waffles, she was always late, because she had to make sure that every little square was buttered and syruped before she'd eat any. Josephine had watched her.

Josephine stood on one foot, then the other, waiting for Sarah—spinning her lunch box around and around in her hands. At last, far up the hill, she saw the door of Sarah's house open, and Sarah came running out, slipping and sliding on the leaves as she made her way down the steep sidewalk. Just as Josie had suspected, Sarah had a drop of syrup on the front of her shirt.

"Mother's taking the piano bench to a repairman today and he's going to tell her how much it will cost," Sarah said.

Josephine didn't tell her about the letter to Greg Maloney. She would keep it a wonderful surprise. As soon as he sent the money, she'd go up to the Prescotts' and say to Sarah

"Put out your hands,
close your eyes,
And I will give you
a big surprise."

Then she'd put the money in Sarah's hands.

Halfway through arithmetic that afternoon, however—division problems—Josephine began to worry that perhaps the bill would be a lot more than seventy-five dollars. Maybe she should have waited to see how much it cost, and *then* written the letter.

"Why don't you come over to my house?" Josephine heard Kimberly Evans ask Sarah when the bell rang at three. "You hardly ever come over anymore."

"She can't," Josie said quickly. "We've got things to do."

"I wasn't asking you, I was asking Sarah," Kimberly said, and waited.

"Well, I don't know. . . ." Sarah hesitated.

"Come on!" Kimberly said brightly, her yellow curls bobbing about on her head. "We could make fudge or something."

For a moment Josie thought that Sarah might say yes. For a moment she even wished Kimberly would invite *her*. But both she and Sarah were waiting for news of the piano bench, so she wasn't surprised when Sarah said finally, "I can't, Kimberly. Not today."

"Okay for *you*!" Kimberly said crossly, and stalked out of the room.

"Maybe we could make fudge at my house," Josie said, never having made fudge in her life.

"Oh, it's all right," Sarah said. They went outside. As they started up the sidewalk, she nudged Josie and said, "Know what Kimberly gave me for my ninth birthday?"

Josephine shook her head.

"A Barbie doll," said Sarah.

"Ugh!" said Josie, and then they were laughing, even better best friends than before. When someone tells you secrets, she's a best friend for sure!

They took a long time going home that afternoon,

kicking at the leaves on the sidewalk and holding up their arms everytime the wind blew and more leaves rained down on them.

"It's raining, it's pouring,
The old man is snoring. . . ."

Josie sang, a yellow leaf stuck on the side of her head.

There were trees behind Sarah's house, as far as the girls could see, because the hill kept on going once it got to Sarah's. On the other side of Webster Springs there were hills too. You came down a long, winding mountain road to get into town on one side, and you went back up another going out. The leaves were changing color, and Josephine counted sixteen different shades of red and yellow.

At Josephine's, Sarah went on up the hill and Josie walked into the house. She sat down at the old upright piano in the dining room and played "Chopsticks" by herself. "Chopsticks" on the Wellses' old upright didn't sound the same as "Chopsticks" on the Prescotts' grand piano, though. A few minutes later the phone rang.

"Good news, sort of," came Sarah's voice. "The furniture man said he didn't have to replace the piano-bench leg; he could repair it. But it will still cost sixty dollars."

"Well, that's better than seventy-five," Josephine said. "I'll pay thirty and you pay thirty."

But as soon as she hung up, Josephine realized that she had never come close to having thirty dollars before. Oh well, she thought. As soon as Greg Maloney sends the money, I'll pay my part of it and Sarah's too, and I'll send what's left back to Greg.

The next day after school, when Josie came in, her mother was making new curtains on the sewing machine.

"Josephine Ruth, I got a call from Sarah's mother today," she said.

Uh oh, thought Josie.

"About a piano bench," said Mrs. Wells.

Josie swallowed.

"Why didn't you tell me that you and Sarah broke a leg on that bench! What a thing to do in the Prescotts' fancy house! Why, I was so ashamed when she told me! And her a doctor's wife!"

"We didn't mean to," said Josephine. "And we're going to pay to have it fixed."

"I should say so!" Mrs. Wells told her. "Mrs. Prescott said it might be nice if you helped Sarah earn the money, and wanted to know if this was going to be too much for you. She said they had raised Sarah to pay for her own mistakes, and I said we raised you the same way. I wouldn't want her to think that people from Summersville do any different."

"Yes, ma'am," said Josie. If only she'd hear from Greg Maloney!

For the next few days, Josephine asked, "Any mail for me?" as soon as she walked in the house.

"No," Mother would always say, and finally she asked, "Are you expecting a letter from someone?"

"Oh, maybe," Josephine told her.

"Josephine Ruth, you're not in any other trouble with the Prescotts, are you?"

"No, ma'am," Josie said. "That piano bench is trouble enough."

On Friday, however, when she came inside, she happened to say, "Any letter yet from Greg?"

"From *Greg*?" said Vernon. "Uh, oh! Josie's got a boyfriend!"

"I do *not*!" said Josephine. "I'm just waiting for a letter, that's all."

Another week went by. Every day Vernon teased her about a boyfriend, and every day there was still no mail for Josie.

Maybe her letter to Greg Maloney got lost. Maybe she should have asked her dad how to address the envelope. But then he would have wanted to know why she was writing to the quarterback, and if she'd told him, the letter would never have been mailed.

"Josephine," said Sarah, as they walked to school the following Monday, "Mom wants to know when we're going to pay her the sixty dollars, and how we're going to earn it, and how come I don't play with Kimberly anymore."

"Tell her you haven't got time for Kimberly—we're going to be working hard to earn that money."

"How?" asked Sarah.

"I'll think of something," said Josie, while her heart beat loud beneath her sweater.

Chapter Three

"Wanted"

On Saturday the girls roller-skated down the long sidewalk that stretched between Sarah's house and the cross street below Josie's. They liked to stand side by side, holding hands, and then—at a "go" from Josephine—begin to roll. Their skates picked up speed as they went down the steep hill, so that the *click . . . click*, as they crossed the cracks in the sidewalk, became *click, click, click, click*, and by the time they turned sharply at the corner, they were both screaming at the top of their lungs, and usually ended up in a heap by a lilac bush. This time, however, they managed to round the corner and keep going until their skates stopped of their own accord.

They sat down on the curb and let their legs dangle over the edge into the street below them.

"I can't think of a thing to do except borrow the money from my sister," Sarah said.

"But then we'd owe sixty dollars to *her*!" said Josephine.

"I know. With interest too. Caroline said she'd charge six dollars just for loaning it to us."

"That's even worse," said Josephine. "No, we've got to earn it. Why don't we put up Job Wanted posters? Do you have any school pictures left from third grade?"

"Yes, but mine were awful!"

"Mine too, but they'd be good enough for posters. Bring all you can find and come on down to my house with your Elmer's glue."

That afternoon the girls sat on the floor of Josephine's bedroom with pieces of cardboard that Josephine's father brought home from work. Mr. Wells had a job in a video store, and every month new posters were put up advertising the latest movies. All the old posters came home to Josephine, and she used the backs of them to draw pictures.

This time, however, Josephine took a black waterproof felt-tipped pen and wrote WANTED in big letters at the top of the first poster. Underneath, she and Sarah each pasted one of their school pictures, and beneath the pictures they wrote: SITTING JOBS. WE SIT PETS OR PLANTS. Then they printed their names and phone numbers.

"I don't know," Josephine said, holding the poster out and looking at it. "I look sort of cross-eyed. I look like the Witch of Wellington Wake."

WANTED
Sitting Jobs.
We Sit pets or
plants.
call
call

"The *what?*"

"It was the name of a story our teacher read to us back in Summersville. The Witch of Wellington Wake was the most evil person in the village, and when she died, everyone was glad. The corn grew again and the milk didn't sour. Only they celebrated too soon, because her ghost came back to take care of some unfinished business, and the ghost was even worse than she was."

Sarah stopped printing. "What did it do?"

"Well, babies started to disappear, and any child who looked the ghost straight in the face was gone the next day."

Sarah shrieked delightedly. "*Then* what?"

"I don't know. I had to leave early for patrol duty and didn't get to hear the end of it."

"Oh, Josie!" wailed Sarah. "*Make up* an end to it, then."

Josephine thought for a moment. "Till one day," she said mysteriously, "the ghost looked at itself in the mirror, and disappeared."

Sarah grinned. "Did the babies and children come back?"

"Nope."

"Why not?"

"Nobody ever found where they went."

"What kind of story is that?"

"Unfinished business," said Josie. The girls laughed again.

"That's one reason I like you," Sarah said. "You make me laugh."

"What's another reason?" Josie asked, pleased.

"Oh, there are lots," Sarah said, and went back to her printing.

"Am I your best friend?" Josie wanted to know.

"Sure."

"You're best, *best* friend?"

"What kind is that?"

"You like a best, *best* friend so much you don't need any others," Josie told her.

Sarah thought it over. "I guess so," she said.

They made five posters. Then they took a hammer and tacked them up on five different telephone poles around their neighborhood. After that, they went back to Josephine's house and waited for the phone to ring.

They played two games of old maid. They counted all the buttons in Josephine's button collection. Then they got out a box of old Halloween masks and tried them on, but the phone still didn't ring.

Vernon came in from playing basketball over at the school.

"Boy, I just saw your pictures!" he said. "They look like those 'Wanted' posters in the post office."

Josie made a face.

"You'll scare people away," Vernon went on. "You'll be the last two girls in Webster Springs that anyone would want to call."

Just then the phone rang. Vernon answered.

"Yeah?" he said. Then, "yeah?" again. And finally, "It's for you," he said to Josephine, looking surprised.

"Hello?" said Josephine. "Why, yes, we will sit anything at all." She grinned first at Vernon, who slunk back off to the kitchen, and then at Sarah, who was jumping up and down. "Fish?" Josephine and Sarah stared at each other. "Of course, we'll feed your fish for you, Mrs. Murphy."

When she hung up, she and Sarah danced around and around, shrieking. "A job! A job! We've got a job!"

"How much?" asked Vernon from the kitchen.

"A dollar a day," said Josephine.

"For how many days?" asked Vernon.

"Four," Josephine told him.

"Four dollars. Big deal!" said Vernon.

"Only fifty-six more to earn," said Josephine. "Let's go."

They went down to the corner and turned right. The hill was so steep that the sidewalk, after they turned, was about four feet higher than the street alongside it. They counted off houses until they came to the fifth from the corner, and that was Mrs. Murphy's.

"I'm going to Ohio for a few days," the woman told them, "and I want someone who will feed my fish and bring in my newspaper."

"We're the best fish-sitters in the world," Josephine said.

"And we won't forget your paper," Sarah promised.

There was a large tank along one wall in Mrs. Murphy's living room, with lots of fish inside it, a light over the tank, a heater in the water, and a little tube that brought in bubbles of air.

"These are my babies," said Mrs. Murphy proudly, and called off the names of her fish: "Samantha, Nirvana, Albert, Prince Charlie, Imogene, Duchess . . ." The names went on and on. Josephine and Sarah exchanged glances and listened politely.

Mrs. Murphy loved to talk. She told them what the temperature of the water should be, the importance of the light, and the amount of food to give the fish at each feeding. She even told them how she had once saved the life of a goldfish by putting it in a little pan of salt water and giving it aspirin.

"But I don't expect you to have any trouble," she said. "All you have to do is give them a pinch of food in the morning, a pinch in the afternoon, and make sure the light is on and the heater's working."

"Easy," said Sarah, and Josie nodded.

Five minutes later they were on their way home with Mrs. Murphy's house key on a ribbon securely around Josephine's neck.

At the dinner table that evening, Mr. Wells said, "If you girls want to earn more money, Josie, you can clean out the basement."

"How much?"

"Three dollars."

"For a whole basement?"

"Take it or leave it," said her father.

"Well, maybe," said Josie.

"Get Caroline Prescott over here to help you," said Clyde. "The way she dresses in school, I'll bet she never had to clean a basement in her life."

"They probably make the butler do it," Vernon snickered.

"They don't have a butler," said Josie.

"Well, if they did, they'd make him do it," said Vernon.

On Monday, Sarah came by early because the girls were to feed Mrs. Murphy's fish before school. They went up the steps to Mrs. Murphy's door, picked up the newspaper, turned the key in the lock, and checked to see that the light over the fish tank, the heater in the water, and the air tube were all working properly.

Sarah gave the fish exactly one pinch of fish food, just as Mrs. Murphy had said. Then they went back out, locked the door, and went to school.

Kimberly hung around Sarah's desk before class began. She had a little bag of M&M's and was giving all the yellow ones to Sarah. Josie walked over.

"What's that key?" Kimberly asked when she saw it around Josie's neck. "Your house key?"

"It's not mine," said Josie proudly, and grinned at Sarah.

Sarah grinned back. "It's a customer's. We've got a business."

"Just you two?" Kimberly asked.

"Just us," said Josie.

Kimberly took the rest of the M&M's back to her seat and gave them to Ellen Ann, who sat beside her.

After school Josephine and Sarah fed Mrs. Murphy's fish again, then went up to the Prescotts' to play. They collected a big pile of leaves under the tree in the backyard, then climbed up the maple and jumped down into the heap, scattering leaves all over the place. Afterward, lying on their backs, their arms and legs spread, they were thinking about going over to Josephine's to clean the basement when Mrs. Prescott came to the back door.

"If you girls rake the yard and bag the leaves, I'll pay you four dollars," she said.

Josephine looked around. It was a big yard. There were lots and lots of leaves. She looked at Sarah.

"I guess so," Sarah told her mother.

Somehow cleaning basements and raking leaves didn't seem nearly as much fun as feeding fish, but money was money, so the girls got rakes and began. If Josephine had three dollars of her own and Sarah had two, that made five dollars. Another four for feeding fish was nine. Three dollars for cleaning a basement made twelve. Four dollars for raking leaves was sixteen dollars. Sixty dollars to pay for a piano-bench leg was still a long way off.

It took them an hour to rake the leaves into three great piles, and then they set to work stuffing them into plastic bags.

"You know what?" said Josephine, staring up at the mountain behind the Prescotts' home as dusk settled around them. "No matter how much we rake, there are always going to be leaves here. Every time the wind blows, the leaves come down from the mountain. I'll bet there are a million billion leaves up there, all waiting to come down in your yard."

Sarah looked too. The wind blew. Leaves came tumbling down from high up in the air, all parachuting right toward the Prescotts' backyard.

"It's okay," Sarah's mother called. "You raked up the leaves that were already there, so here's your four dollars. Every time you rake again, you get another four."

"Yea!" yelled Josephine. "Come on, leaves! Keep coming!"

As the girls were dragging the plastic bags out to the curb, however, Sarah's sister came home from high school.

"Sarah, why did you put up those ridiculous posters?" Caroline asked.

"I didn't think they were so ridiculous," said Sarah.

"Well, they are now," said Caroline. "Go look."

Josephine and Sarah ran down the hill to the telephone pole at the bottom. There was a poster. And there were the photographs of Sarah and Josephine, each with a mustache.

With Josie in the lead, they ran to the next telephone pole and the next. And on all five posters, Josephine Wells and Sarah Prescott had big black mustaches painted just above their upper lips.

Chapter Four

Good-bye, Albert

"I'll bet it was Vernon!" said Josephine angrily. "Who else would be mean enough to do that?"

But when the girls went back to Josie's house and told, Vernon said, "I might have *thought* about doing it, but I never really *would*." And Josephine figured that was true.

"It must have been Kimberly Evans, then," she said. "Kimberly and Ellen Ann. They were whispering and laughing at us at recess. That just shows what kind of a friend *Kimberly* is."

"She never did anything like that before," said Sarah.

"Well, people change," Josie told her.

Mrs. Wells walked down to the corner with them and showed them how, if they rubbed hard on the photos with Kleenex, most of the mustache came off. Then the pictures just looked like two girls with dirty faces.

"People will understand," said Josie's mother. "It won't keep them from hiring you if they really need a pet- or plant-sitter."

She was right, because after Sarah went home, she called Josephine to say that someone had phoned the Prescotts' number. "We've got another customer!" she said happily.

"What do we sit this time? More fish?" Josie asked.

"A rubber plant," said Sarah. "For two weeks."

"A *rubber* plant?" Josephine turned toward her family, who were all sitting at the kitchen table eating spareribs.

"That's a plant that grows rubber bands," Father teased.

"Naw, rubber pants," Clyde chortled.

"Rubber duckies," Vernon added.

"Oh, for goodness sake!" said Josephine's mother. "It's a big plant with large thick leaves, *that's* what it is."

"What are they talking about, Josie?" came Sarah's voice over the phone.

"About what a rubber plant is, and it sounds just fine to me," Josephine told her.

The following day it was Sarah who had a key to wear around her neck. It was fun going to school, each of them with a key around her neck; fun to have real jobs.

"Could I go with you later to water the rubber plant?" Ellen Ann asked when she heard about it. She was a tall, thin girl, who Josie might have chosen for a best friend if she didn't already have Sarah. "I could be in your business with you."

"We're the only ones who are allowed in Mr. Kellerman's house," Sarah said. "And besides," she added, when Kimberly came over to hear what the three girls were talking about, "we wouldn't take you two anyway, because we know who drew those mustaches on our pictures."

"*What* mustaches?" Ellen Ann asked, but Kimberly only laughed.

"Serves you right," she said. "You're so stuck-up you won't let anyone else join your business."

Now Josephine was really angry. "You *did* draw those mustaches, Kimberly. We wouldn't let you join our business now for anything!"

"Well, maybe we don't *want* to join!" said Kimberly. "Maybe we've got something better! Come on, Ellen Ann." And the two girls walked away.

Josephine watched them go. "What do you suppose she meant by that?"

"I don't know, but now I'm *really* glad I didn't stay best friends with her, Josie."

"*Are* you, Sarah? Really?" Josie asked anxiously.

"Really," said Sarah. And they were even better best friends than they were before.

After school the girls went to Mr. Kellerman's house to water the rubber plant. They were also to bring in the mail, put the lids back on the trash cans after the garbage truck had come by, and turn on a different light every evening to make the house look as though someone were there. Two dollars a day. Two dollars a day for fourteen days meant twenty-eight dollars!

Just as Mother had said, the rubber plant was huge. It sat in the hallway at the foot of the stairs, and its top leaves reached as far as the seventh step. The leaves were thick and rubbery-looking, and it seemed like the kind of tree that should be in a jungle with purple parrots in it.

Sarah added water to keep the soil moist, as Mr. Kellerman had instructed, and Josie sprayed the leaves with mist. The girls carefully locked the door after them before they went off to feed Mrs. Murphy's fish.

This time Sarah checked the light and the air tube and the heater to see that everything was on and working, while Josephine gave the fish their pinch of fish food. They stood beside the tank watching as the fish darted to the surface, their O-shaped mouths nibbling at the flakes that floated on top.

"You know," said Josephine, after a moment, "I don't think Albert looks so good." She pointed to the next-largest fish at the bottom.

"How do you know it's Albert?"

"I remember the stripe on his back when Mrs. Murphy told us their names. See how he just sits there? He's not even eating."

"He's too fat anyway," said Sarah.

The next morning, however, when the girls stopped by Mrs. Murphy's house, Albert was no better, and when they came again after school, he was definitely worse. This time he was on top of the water, swimming on his side. He swam for a while, then floated awhile.

"What are we going to *do?*" Sarah wondered.

Josephine wished that she had asked more questions when Mrs. Murphy was chattering on about sick fish. "Salt water," Josephine said.

So the girls went into Mrs. Murphy's kitchen, got a saucepan from the cupboard, and dipped up half a pan of water from the fish tank.

"How much salt?" Sarah asked, holding the shaker above the pan.

"A couple of shakes," said Josephine, only guessing.

They stirred the water with a spoon. Josephine found a tea strainer in Mrs. Murphy's drawer and gently scooped Albert, the ailing fish, into the strainer, then put him in the pan of salted water. Albert swam around once, then turned over again on his side.

"She also said something about aspirin," Sarah remembered.

The girls went up to Mrs. Murphy's bathroom and got some aspirin from the medicine cabinet.

"How much?" Sarah asked again, holding an aspirin over the saucepan.

SAL
ASPIRIN

"Just break off a little corner," Josie suggested.

Sarah rubbed a little piece of aspirin between her finger and thumb so that a fine powder drifted down onto the water's surface. They even pushed some of it close to Albert's face, but it didn't look as though the fish was eating any.

"Eat, Albert, eat!" Josephine begged.

The fish went on floating.

"Maybe the aspirin soaks in through the gills," Sarah said.

The next problem was how to keep Albert warm enough. There was no heater for the saucepan, so the girls put the pan on Mrs. Murphy's desk, turned on the desk lamp, and left, hoping for the best.

They didn't say much as they went back around the corner to Josephine's house, because they were both worried about Albert. But when they reached the Wellses' porch, Josie's mother came to the door.

"Good news!" she said. "Mrs. Caldwell up the block is going to visit her sister in Tennessee. She doesn't know how long she'll be gone, but she wants you to let her cat in every morning and feed it, then feed it again at night and let it out. Two dollars a day."

"Wow!" said Josephine and Sarah together. Things were definitely looking up. They were becoming known around Webster Springs! They'd be famous! *Josie and Sarah, the Wonder Girls!* Maybe they wouldn't have to clean the basement after all.

"When do we start?" Josephine asked her mother.

"This evening. Mrs. Caldwell came by and left the key."

Josephine slipped the key around her neck along with Mrs. Murphy's key. She was so excited she almost forgot about Albert.

The girls went up the block to Mrs. Caldwell's home. Inside was a very hungry cat, Measles, waiting for his dinner. There was a note on the refrigerator about what to do, so the girls gave Measles half a cup of dry food, filled his water dish, cleaned his litter box, and then, when the cat was through eating, let him out. He followed Josephine home.

"What should I do, Mother?" she asked.

"Just let him be. Cats do that. He'll get tired of waiting on the porch after awhile and wander off, but I'm sure he'll be back at Mrs. Caldwell's tomorrow morning wanting his breakfast."

That night Josephine did her arithmetic problems and read a chapter in her science book, but all the while she was studying, Measles sat on the front porch and meowed.

At five the next morning, when Josephine woke up, she didn't hear Measles, but she was worried about Albert. Was he all right now? Would they be able to put him back in the tank with the other fish before Mrs. Murphy came home the following day?

It was too early to call Sarah, so Josephine got up quietly and dressed for school. Then she crept down the hall and went outside.

Measles had been asleep all night on the glider. He got up and stretched when he saw Josephine, glad to have company. He came over and rubbed against her leg.

"Not yet," said Josephine. "I'm going to check on Albert."

They went down the block and around the corner to Mrs. Murphy's house in the early-morning darkness.

"No!" Josephine said sternly, shaking her finger at Measles. "You stay out here."

Measles crouched down on the steps.

Josephine unlocked the door and went inside. With her heart pounding, she hurried into the dining room and over to Mrs. Murphy's desk, where the light was still on.

Albert was lying on his side. He had turned from light orange to pale pink. He was not moving at all.

"A-Albert!" said Josephine. Gently she touched him with one finger. The fish did not move. His gills did not move. Josephine swished him around in the saucepan. Albert just rolled over on his back and floated belly up. It was Good-bye, Albert.

Chapter Five

Missing Measles

Josephine and Sarah stood on the playground at recess and tried to decide what to do.

"See?" said Kimberly Evans, who was twisting around and around in one of the swings, then turning the other way and letting the swing spin. "You don't even know anything about fish. I've had lots of them. You should have asked me."

"If we'd asked *you*, Albert probably would have died sooner," Josie said. "You'd love to ruin our business."

Kimberly came to a stop on the swings. "You just came here to start trouble, Josephine Wells!" she said. "Sarah and I used to be good friends till you moved to Webster Springs."

Josie looked quickly at Sarah.

"I'd never be friends with someone who went around marking up posters," Sarah told her, and Josie was relieved.

"Can't you take a joke?" asked Kimberly, but Josie and Sarah walked away. They had worries enough with Albert, and wondered what they should do with him. Josie didn't think they should leave him floating around in a saucepan, and they especially did not want Mrs. Murphy to find him there when she came home the next day.

"We ought to give Albert a proper funeral," Sarah said finally.

Josephine swallowed. She had been thinking of just flushing him down the toilet herself. "You mean with prayers and everything?" she asked.

"Well, we've got to say *something*," Sarah told her.

"Where will we bury him?"

"I don't know. We had a canary once, and when it died, Mom said to bury it beneath a rosebush so his body would help fertilize it, and every time the roses bloomed, we'd think of High C. That was his name."

Josephine thought about Mrs. Murphy's yard. There wasn't any grass. In fact, all but the brick sidewalk was covered with ivy—no bushes anywhere. "We could bury him beneath Mr. Kellerman's rubber plant. It would fertilize the plant and be doing *something* some good," she suggested.

"But what will we tell Mrs. Murphy?"

"I'll think of something," said Josephine. That was beginning to be her favorite line.

They were very quiet that afternoon when they made their rounds. First they went to Mrs. Caldwell's, where Josie had fed Measles that morning and locked him in. They fed the cat again, emptied his litter box, and let him out for the night. He promptly followed along behind them as they went to Mrs. Murphy's, but the girls were careful not to let him in.

Albert looked even more dead than he had that morning. Sarah got the tea strainer and they lifted him out of the saucepan and wrapped him in a tissue. Josie had tears in her eyes, but not so much for Albert. It was their job she felt saddest about. A dead fish certainly didn't help business any.

When the other fish had been fed and checked, they went on to Mr. Kellerman's for the fish funeral ceremony. They put away the trash cans, picked up Mr. Kellerman's mail, and went inside.

Sarah took a teaspoon and dug a little grave in the dirt beneath the towering rubber plant. Josephine placed Albert, wrapped in his shroud of Kleenex, inside the hole. They crouched there beside the plant.

"Do you know any good words to say?" asked Sarah.

Josephine tried her best, but it was hard to think of what to say for a dead fish.

"And they swam and they swam
All over the dam"

she said finally.

"What?"

"It's the only poem I know about a fish. Do you know any?"

Sarah thought. At last she bowed her head and said:

"Fishie, fishie, in the brook,
Daddy caught him with a hook,
Mother fried him in the pan,
Johnny ate him like a man."

Josie stared. "That's *awful*, Sarah!"

"Well, it's all I know. Let's just say he was a good fish, the other fish loved him, and then cover him up."

She took the teaspoon and dropped some of the dirt back over the fish. Then she handed the spoon to Josephine, and Josie covered the rest of the grave. The rubber plant didn't need watering yet, so the girls turned off one light, turned on another, locked the door, and walked sadly home.

Josie told her family about it at dinner that night. "How am I going to tell Mrs. Murphy that Albert died?" she said, pushing her meat loaf from one side of her plate to the other, then flopping it over with her fork.

"Just tell her the truth," said Father. "It wasn't your fault, Josie. You did everything you knew to do for a sick fish."

"A special fish," said Josie. "A fish named Albert—her favorite."

"Even favorite fish have to die sometime," Father told her.

Sarah came down early the next morning to make their rounds before school. The other fish were doing fine at Mrs. Murphy's. But when the girls reached Mrs. Caldwell's house to let the cat in and feed it, Measles wasn't there.

"Oh, no!" Josephine cried. "Don't tell me we've lost Measles! A dead fish and now a lost cat?"

"All we need is to find the rubber plant on its side when we go to Mr. Kellerman's this afternoon," said Sarah.

"Here kitty, kitty, kitty!" Josephine called, walking around the house, looking behind all the bushes, even under the porch. But there was no cat.

The day passed much too quickly at school. The girls were in no hurry to talk to Mrs. Murphy when she got home that afternoon. It was harder still to keep their minds on their work.

"Josephine, are you paying attention?" the teacher asked as she explained a long division problem on the blackboard.

"No, ma'am . . . I mean, yes, ma'am," Josephine said, turning quickly from the window, hoping to see Measles out on the playground.

There were giggles from the back of the room and Josie knew it was Kimberly Evans. Kimberly Evans and Ellen Ann.

When the bell rang at three, Josie and Sarah had to force their feet down the sidewalk and up the hill toward Mrs. Murphy's house. The woman was waiting for them on her front porch. Her eyes were red, and Josephine wondered if she'd been crying. Josie herself was never that fond of fish, but she could understand how someone might feel about a special pet. *Any* pet. Even Albert.

"What happened?" Mrs. Murphy asked softly.

"We don't know," Josie said miserably. "We're terribly sorry, but when we came to check one morning, Albert looked sick."

"He was swimming on his side," said Sarah.

"When we came back that evening he was even sicker," Josephine went on. "We remembered what you said, so we put him in a saucepan with some salt water and a little bit of aspirin, but the next morning he was dead."

Mrs. Murphy dabbed at her eyes. She said that Albert had been the favorite of all her fish, named after her husband, and how she should never have gone off to Ohio. But finally she turned to the girls and said, "I'm sure you did all you could to save him, and maybe I wouldn't have been able to do any more. So I shall just have to bury him and forget it."

Josephine and Sarah looked at each other.

"Where is he?" Mrs. Murphy asked.

"Well . . . uh . . . we sort of held a funeral for him

ourselves," said Josephine. "We thought that's what you would have wanted." Boy, was she glad she hadn't flushed him down the toilet.

"Where?" asked Mrs. Murphy.

Josephine swallowed. "Under Mr. Kellerman's rubber plant."

"What?" cried Mrs. Murphy.

"We . . . we wanted his body to go where it would do some good. I mean, fertilize something, so we . . ."

"I don't think Mr. Kellerman would appreciate that one bit. He is very fussy about his house and plants," said Mrs. Murphy, buttoning up her sweater. "Let's go get Albert."

They passed Mrs. Caldwell's house on the way, and both Josie and Sarah looked to see if Measles was waiting on the porch. He wasn't. Josephine walked on silently. She was really worried. Mrs. Murphy was sniffling again over Albert, and Sarah was on the verge of crying over Measles. Maybe the cat had really run away. Worse yet, maybe he'd been stolen—catnapped—or run over. Poisoned, even!

Suddenly Sarah grabbed Josie's arm and pointed. They had just reached Mr. Kellerman's house, and there was Mr. Kellerman standing out on his steps, looking very upset.

"He was supposed to be gone for two weeks!" Josie said.

"What happened?" Mr. Kellerman asked as the girls came up the sidewalk with Mrs. Murphy.

"What do you mean?" asked Josie, staring.

"I got only as far as Toledo and my business trip was canceled," Mr. Kellerman told them. "So I came back home to find *this*!" He turned and pointed inside the house where the door stood wide open.

Josephine and Sarah stepped cautiously inside, expecting to find the giant rubber plant dead, its leaves shriveled. The plant looked fine, but there was dirt all over the Oriental rug on which it stood.

"*Some*one has been digging around the roots of my beautiful plant," said Mr. Kellerman, "throwing dirt all over my rug."

"But we didn't do it!" Sarah protested. "When we dug the grave, we did it so gently we didn't get a speck of dirt on anything!"

Now Mr. Kellerman was staring. "*What* grave?"

"Mr. Kellerman, I'm afraid that the girls have buried my Albert beneath your rubber plant," said Mrs. Murphy, coming in the open door.

"A-Albert?" said Mr. Kellerman, but Josephine was already down on her knees, poking one finger around in the soil in the rubber plant's pot. There were shreds of Kleenex here and there, but the only thing left of Albert was his backbone and one small piece of his tail.

"Albert?" said Mrs. Murphy sadly, staring down at the hole.

At that moment a ball of yellow came streaking out of the living room, across the Oriental rug, and

out the front door—a streak of yellow with orange spots.

"Measles!" cried Josephine and Sarah together. And then they realized that when they had come to bury Albert, Measles had probably slipped in with them. They had been so upset about the fish that they had forgotten the cat entirely, and Measles, shut up in a strange house overnight, ate the only thing he could find, which was, of course, Albert. For the second time that day, the girls had to explain.

"Do you mean to say there has been a cat in my house overnight?" said Mr. Kellerman. "Do you know I'm allergic to cats?"

"Oh, dear!" said Mrs. Murphy.

"We're sorry," Josie said. "We won't charge you, Mr. Kellerman, and we'll clean up your rug."

Mrs. Murphy paid the girls for their fish-sitting and went home with only Albert's backbone to console her. Josephine and Sarah took Mr. Kellerman's vacuum cleaner and cleaned the dirt off his rug while he watched them, arms folded across his chest.

At least we've still got our cat-sitting job, Josie thought gratefully.

But when they went outside to take Measles home, the cat was gone again.

Chapter Six

The Siamese Twins

"Do people ever go to jail for doing bad work on a job?"

That was what Josie asked her mother the next day.

"Depends on what exactly they do," Mrs. Wells replied. "If you mean stealing something, yes, sometimes they go to jail."

"I mean accidents."

"What have you done now, Josie? I swear, every time you and Sarah get together, you get in trouble all over again."

Josie sadly explained about Albert, the dirt on Mr. Kellerman's rug, and the fact that Measles was missing.

"Well, I don't know, Josie. I can't say it was your fault, but you and Sarah got yourselves into this and now you've got to get yourselves out," her mother said, which wasn't much help at all. "You'd better start looking for that cat."

"We have. We've walked all over the neighbor-hood."

The two girls had paid Mrs. Prescott the sixteen dollars they had saved and collected so far, but there were still forty-four dollars yet to earn.

Measles had not come back. Every morning and every evening the girls went to Mrs. Caldwell's and called, but the cat never came. They left a little dish of food outside on the porch for him, just in case he *was* still around. But it didn't look as though any of the food had been eaten.

They even began to look for a run-over cat. Every time Josephine saw something lying in the street, she held her breath, then let it out again when she dis-covered it was just a paper bag or a box that had been squished. And every morning when she woke up, she wondered what she was going to tell Mrs. Caldwell about her pet.

To make a bad week worse, Kimberly Evans and Ellen Ann seemed to have secrets of their own. At recess, they laughed and whispered over by the fence, and the next thing Josie knew, there were pin pricks all over her and Sarah's pictures on their Job Wanted posters. It made both girls look as though they had pimples.

"Let's don't speak to Kimberly ever again, even if

she speaks first," said Sarah. "Even if she invites us to her birthday party, we won't go! Or to Ellen Ann's either!"

Josie quickly agreed. She had only been to three birthday parties since she was born, and she would have liked to be invited to a party here in Webster Springs. But it was because of her that Sarah and Kimberly weren't best friends anymore, and being friends with Sarah mattered more than anything. Now she and Sarah were best, *best* friends!

There was to be a Halloween party on Friday, though, and that was something to look forward to. It would be given by the fire department for all the children of Webster Springs, and all you needed to get in was a costume.

"You know, Josie," said her father, "you could ask the firemen to make an announcement about Measles while you're there. With all those children looking for him, *some*one should find him."

"Okay," said Josephine. It was a little embarrassing, but she'd do it.

She was going to the Halloween party as a pirate with a black patch over one eye, a red scarf over her head, and a sword on the belt of her jeans.

Sarah was going as a pumpkin, in a large orange bag stuffed with tissue paper that her mother had made for her, and a little orange cap with a stem on it.

Even Vernon was going to the party, dressed as a

transistor radio, which was really a box over his head, an antenna at one end, and knobs at the other.

Clyde said he was too old to go to fire-department parties, and Sarah said that Caroline had said the same thing.

"Maybe you'd have a good time if you had a date," Josie suggested to her brother. "Why don't you ask Caroline Prescott to go?"

"*Her?*" said Clyde. "She's so snooty she doesn't even know I'm around."

So the girls asked Caroline if she'd go to the party if Clyde asked her.

"I wouldn't even go to a car wash with Clyde Wells," said Caroline. "He's always doing stupid things to make me notice him."

"How do you suppose people ever grow up and get married if they all start out like this?" Josie asked Sarah.

On Halloween night Josephine, the pirate, waited for Sarah, the pumpkin, and they walked with Vernon, the transistor radio, down the steep hill to the fire department on the street below. Already they could hear the music.

As soon as they reached the fire station, Vernon went off to be with friends, but Josephine and Sarah didn't mind. In the entrance to the firehouse a strobe light flashed on and off, so that when they walked into the hallway, each girl looked as though she had been captured in a photograph—Josephine with her eye patch, Sarah in her pumpkin-stem cap.

It was spooky inside the main room. Some of the firemen were dressed as zombies, and they went around grabbing children by the shoulders and leading them over to a table of cider and doughnuts. Josephine and Sarah stayed together, laughing at the firemen who did a "zombie dance" to the tunes of a "zombie band."

But children seemed to be gathering at the far end of the room, and when Josie and Sarah went to see what was happening, they saw Kimberly Evans and Ellen Ann in a Siamese-twin cat costume. Each of them was dressed as a black cat, with long white whiskers on their cheeks, and black stockings stuffed with tissue paper for tails. But Kimberly's right leg was in the same leg of the costume as Ellen Ann's left leg, so that it looked like two cats joined together—Siamese-twin cats. They had practiced so that they could walk together, turn together. They even did a little dance together, and everyone clapped.

Josie stole a look at Sarah, and could tell by her eyes that Sarah would have liked to be one of those cats. It *would* have been fun to be dancing out there in front of everyone else, listening to people clap. And later, when Josie asked one of the firemen to announce a missing cat, and he did, Kimberly and Ellen Ann each pretended to be the missing cat, and they wiped their eyes with their paws. Ellen Ann even wiped *her*

eyes with her tail, and everyone laughed again. Josie could hardly stand it.

Kimberly and Ellen Ann won first prize in the costume contest, of course. Sarah won second prize for her pumpkin costume, and Vernon won third. After the prizes were awarded, everyone started for home.

It helped a little that Sarah had won at least something, and she chattered about it as they went up the hill. Josie and Vernon walked to her house with her to make sure she got home okay, but when they started back down, Vernon was angry.

"I worked on that transistor-radio costume for a week, and only won third place!" he said. "It isn't fair! I think they should only give prizes to kids who make the costumes themselves. Those other costumes were made on a sewing machine; anyone could see that."

"Well, I'm glad Sarah won something," said Josie.

"I thought her costume stunk," said Vernon. "I'll bet the maid sewed it for her."

"They don't have a maid," said Josie.

"Well, if they did, the maid would have done it."

When they got in the house, Josie's father asked, "Did they make an announcement about Measles?"

Josie nodded. "But no one told us anything. Two girls were hamming it up in a cat costume, and I don't think anyone really listened to the announcement."

"Well, maybe you're not trying hard enough, Josie. I passed Dr. Prescott on the way to the mailbox this evening, and thought he looked at me a little strangely. We don't want the Prescotts to think that the folks who live down here don't work every bit as hard as the people up on the hill. If I were you, I'd look everywhere there was to look."

"We *have*!" Josephine snapped. "And we go over every day to check Measles' dish. He's never there."

"Well, don't bite my head off," her father said. "But maybe you should put up notices asking if anyone has seen him. You at least want to be able to tell Mrs. Caldwell that you did everything you could."

Sarah came over the next day and the girls spent the afternoon making signs that said MEASLES IS MISSING with a drawing of a cat's face on them. Beneath the cat's face they printed their phone numbers, should anyone happen to see the cat. But Sarah was discouraged.

"I don't think we're *ever* going to earn enough money to pay my mother back," she said. "This is going to go on forever, one problem after another."

Josie tried to think of something cheerful to say. Wasn't that what best, *best* friends were for? Then she remembered the quarterback.

"Maybe we won't have to earn any more," she said mysteriously.

Sarah looked up. "Why not?"

"Because I wrote to Greg Maloney, the millionaire football player from West Virginia, and asked if we could have seventy-five dollars," Josie told her.

"What?" cried Sarah.

Josie explained how Greg Maloney probably had three rosewood grand pianos in his home, and would be glad to help out somebody else from West Virginia.

"Do you really think he'll send the money?"

"Of course," said Josie. "How could he say no to someone from his own state? And I told him we'd pay it back if he wanted, but I'm sure he won't ask."

And as though a sign from heaven, the girls saw Greg Maloney on television when they got back from tacking up their notices. Josephine's father and brothers were watching college football, but during the commercials there was a public-service announcement about giving to the United Way. And there on the screen, with his arms around two children with crutches, was the quarterback, his blue eyes looking right at Josie. He was talking about how sometimes we have to overcome obstacles to reach our goals, but just because it's hard doesn't mean we won't make it. "Give the United Way," he said, and then, smiling down at the two children with crutches, "Life is full of surprises."

Josephine stood transfixed in the doorway. This was a message to her that money was on the way; she was sure of it. Any man who would take time from making millions of dollars just to appear in a public-service announcement with crippled children would certainly answer the letter of a nine-year-old girl in his home state.

"Any day now, Sarah," she whispered. "You wait and see."

Phone calls started coming almost at once about Measles. That was a good sign too. One woman called to say that she saw an orange cat with yellow spots, another called to say that she had seen a yellow cat with orange stripes, and a third called to say that she was sure she had seen Measles, but couldn't remember where.

And then, just after Josie had hung up for the fourth time, a man called to say that he was going on a business trip, that his wife had sprained her ankle, and they needed an experienced dog walker to walk their Great Dane once a day, twice a day on week-ends.

"We're experienced!" Josie said, but did not say at what.

"Good. Would you do it for two-fifty a day, five dollars on Saturdays and Sundays?"

"Of course!" Josie told him, and she and Sarah danced around the kitchen. "See, Sarah? Good things are happening already!"

"Come up to my house and stay all night, Josie," Sarah begged. "Then we can get up early and walk that dog."

Sarah called her mother and asked if she could bring Josie home to stay over, and Mrs. Prescott said yes, as long as they didn't fool around on the piano. They asked Josie's mother if Josephine could stay overnight with Sarah, and Mrs. Wells said yes, if they thought they could behave. And by the time Josie had packed her bag, she was beginning to feel a lot better. She and Sarah would be friends forever, always, for the rest of their lives.

Chapter Seven

Walking Jaws

First the girls roller-skated on the sidewalk until dinnertime. Then they ate the "kabobs" that Mrs. Prescott had made, which were pieces of meat and vegetables on little sticks broiled in the oven. And finally, when Caroline was doing the dishes and Mrs. Prescott was weaving a rug and Dr. Prescott was listening to a Beethoven violin concerto, Sarah and Josie went upstairs.

Sarah's bedroom was the large one on the right side of the house. There were a lot of things to do there—games, a small TV, Sarah's shark-tooth collection, and puzzles, and after one game of *Girl Talk*, the girls practiced doing cartwheels on the braided rug. Until Caroline came in.

"Sarah, what on earth are you doing?" she asked. "It sounds like elephants leaping around. The whole house is shaking." And then, to Josie, "You make almost as much noise as your brother!"

The girls stopped, but when Caroline had gone, Josie said, "It seems as though every time they bawl you out about something, *I'm* here."

"Oh, Caroline's always like that," Sarah told her. "You worry too much, Josie."

Maybe so, Josie thought, but she wanted the Prescotts to like her. Sarah had been the first girl—the *only* girl, at the time—to make friends with Josephine when she moved up from Summersville. For a while the other girls had just watched her from across the classroom; hadn't even asked her to sit with them at lunch. And now, her wish had come true. Sarah was not only her friend, but her best, *best* friend.

Later, Sarah's mother brought up some milk and cinnamon toast, with cinnamon and sugar on both sides, and it began to look as though the evening would turn out all right. But Sarah, strangely, had grown very quiet. "Do dreams ever mean anything, Josie?" she asked finally.

"I don't know. What did you dream?"

"I had a horrible dream about Measles last night. I dreamed that Kimberly killed him."

Josie sucked in her breath. "That's terrible!" she said. "How did she do it?"

"Drowned him. There was a lake or something outside my window and I thought I saw something floating in it, and when I opened the door to see, Measles's body was lying on the doormat, dripping wet, and Kimberly was standing out under a tree laughing. I think it's the worst dream I ever had in my life. I've been trying not to think about it all day."

Josie had goose bumps on her arms. "She may draw mustaches on pictures, but Kimberly wouldn't really do something like that, would she, Sarah?"

"I don't know. Kimberly moved here two years ago from Kentucky. I don't know what they do in Kentucky. No one liked her at first except me."

"Why not?"

"Oh, I don't know. She didn't smile much, and wore her hair sort of funny."

Josie swallowed. She wondered if anyone had felt that way about her when she had first come to Webster Springs. She probably hadn't smiled much either. She'd been so worried about making friends she hadn't *felt* much like smiling. And maybe her hair or her shoes or her clothes or her lunch box was a little bit different from the others. People living in different towns just do things differently sometimes.

"Anyway," Sarah added, "I'm glad *we're* best friends now. You're the best friend I ever had, Josie."

That made Josephine feel much, much better. "You're mine too," she said.

Even so, Josie didn't sleep very well that night. She was in Sarah's big bedroom with the twin beds and white ruffles and a bird mobile hanging from the ceiling that caught the beam of the streetlight as the birds moved back and forth in the breeze. She was thinking about Sarah's dream. *Did* dreams ever mean that something awful was about to happen? Was it possible that she and Sarah would get up the next morning and find Measles's dead body lying on the front porch?

When daylight came, she simply had to find out. She looked over at Sarah; Sarah was sleeping soundly. Josie got out of bed, tiptoed silently out in the hall in her pajamas, and down the stairs.

She was just about to open the front door when she saw the doorknob turning all by itself, and before she could turn and run, the door opened and there stood Dr. Prescott in his bathrobe, carrying the morning newspaper.

"Well!" he said. "What are you doing up so early?"

Josephine could not think of an answer. Everything she thought of seemed wrong. She could not tell him that she had come to see whether or not there was a dead cat on the front doorstep. And suddenly she wheeled around and ran back upstairs to Sarah's bedroom without a word, which was even worse.

Because when she and Sarah came down to breakfast later, she overheard Dr. Prescott talking to Sarah's mother in the kitchen.

"What in the world are those girls up to?" he was saying. "When I came in with the paper this morning, I found Josephine prowling around the front hall. I asked, but she wouldn't tell me what she was doing."

Josephine's cheeks flamed bright red. They probably thought she was stealing. People thought all kinds of things about folks from Summersville.

UNIVERSITY
OF

"Good morning, girls," Sarah's mother said when she saw them. "French toast or pancakes, Josephine?"

Josephine couldn't stand it any longer. "*Search* me," she said.

Dr. and Mrs. Prescott turned and stared at her. So did Sarah.

"What?" said Mrs. Prescott.

"I wasn't prowling around your house and I didn't steal anything," Josephine went on.

Dr. Prescott's mouth fell open. "Why, of course you didn't steal anything, Josephine. I never said you did!"

"I—I just wanted to check the front porch to see if—if—"

Sarah finished for her. "To see if there was a dead cat on the doormat," she said, motioning Josie to the chair next to her. "It was a dream I had, and I think Josie was checking it out."

"Listen, you girls," said Mrs. Prescott. "I know you're upset that Measles is missing, but it seems to me you've done everything you can to find him. Now try some of my blueberry pancakes, and see if you don't feel better."

Mrs. Prescott's friendly voice alone made Josephine feel better, and she ate four large pancakes. Dr. Prescott made a point of smiling at her and asking about her family. He even asked if she would like to stay for lunch, but Josie said she had to be getting home.

"Not until we walk the dog," said Sarah.

"*What* dog?" Josephine asked, and then she remembered. They still had a job!

The people who owned the dog, the Garsons, lived seven blocks away. To get there, the girls walked along a high sidewalk four feet above street level until they came to the house.

"Now all we have to do is walk him, they said," Sarah told Josie as they went up on the porch. "We don't have to feed him or anything." She rang the bell.

There was a noise from inside. Josephine couldn't tell if it was a bellow, a roar, or a howl, but it sounded like a seal, a lion, and a wolf all howling and braying at once. And suddenly the largest dog that Josephine had seen in her life leaped up on the inside of the glass door, and both girls tumbled backward, Sarah sliding to the floor.

A woman appeared behind the huge beast and opened the door just a crack.

"He's really very gentle," she said. "He just gets excited when we have company. Are you the dog walkers? Come on in."

Josephine stood rooted to the spot. Sarah remained on her knees.

"Look," said Mrs. Garson. "He wants to be friends."

Josephine peered through the glass. The huge animal was sitting now on his haunches, with one paw extended. Even sitting down, he came up as high as Josephine's shoulder.

"You *are* the girls my husband spoke with, aren't you?" the woman said. "Then please come in. I've sprained my ankle, and it hurts to stand here."

Josephine looked at the dog. He did seem to look friendly, and she had just taken a step forward when the dog yawned. His mouth looked like a cavern. His teeth looked like butcher knives. But she had told Mr. Garson that she would do it, so she put one foot in front of the other and found herself inside the house.

"His name is Jaws, and he's a Great Dane," said Mrs. Garson. "Gentle Jaws, we call him."

It was like walking into a lion's den, Josephine thought. She could hear the dog breathing. She could smell his wet breath. Any moment she expected to find herself flat on her back with the dog's teeth at her throat.

She and Sarah went into the living room and sat down together on the couch. Jaws sat down at their feet—first his back legs went down, then his front legs, then his body, and finally his head, resting there on his paws.

"He's such a *big* dog!" Mrs. Garson said, "and he's just *got* to be walked every day or he goes crazy. We have a good strong leash, and if you wrap it firmly around your hand and keep a good grip on it, you shouldn't have any trouble. Do you want to try?"

It was like asking, Do you want to jump out of a

plane without a parachute? Josephine thought, but how could they keep their job if they turned pets down?

"Yes, ma'am," she told Mrs. Garson. "How far should we walk him?"

"Keep him out at least twenty minutes," the woman said. "And hold onto the leash tightly!"

She got a leash from the closet. Jaws sat up. She fastened it to his collar. Jaws rose to his feet. She handed the leash to Josephine, and suddenly the dog took off toward the front door, whirling Josie around, dragging her across the carpet, and leaping up on the door.

"He's *so* happy!" said Mrs. Garson, and she opened the door. "You're sure you can handle him, now?"

Josephine didn't even have time to say "Sarah!" She didn't even have time to say "help!" The next thing she knew she was leaping down the porch steps behind Jaws as he galloped across the front yard and rushed headlong down the sidewalk. Sarah caught up with her at the corner, and it was only by holding on to the leash together that they were able to keep the huge dog from charging across the street.

They waited until their hearts stopped pounding.

"Well," Josephine breathed at last, "we're back in business."

Chapter Eight

More Trouble

It was not clear, as Josephine and Sarah went galloping down the street after Jaws, whether they were walking the dog or the Great Dane was walking them.

At one point, when a squirrel went scampering over someone's lawn, Jaws gave such a lunge that Josephine tumbled forward, Jaws pulling her along behind him on her knees. Sarah managed to wrap the leash around a tree and the monster stopped and sat down, panting.

Josephine and Sarah were panting too. "How long does this job last?" Josephine asked.

"Till Mr. Garson comes back or Mrs. Garson's ankle gets better or we die of exhaustion," Sarah told her.

They finally worked out a system. Josephine wrapped part of the leash around her hand, Sarah wrapped some more of the leash around hers, and

when they came to a corner they both yelled "stop!" If Jaws didn't stop, they held on to a signpost.

By the time the twenty minutes were up, they had almost got the hang of it, so that when they returned Jaws to the Garsons', they looked as though they knew what they were doing. The dog turned toward Josie, his long red tongue out, and gave her a big wet slurp along one cheek and up over her eye.

"I was a little worried there for a while that you girls couldn't handle him, but it looks as though you got along fine," Mrs. Garson said, and paid them two-and-a-half dollars.

Two dollars and fifty cents a day for walking the monster dog, and five dollars on weekends would certainly help pay for the piano bench. If only they could keep on getting jobs like this.

On the way home they checked Mrs. Caldwell's house again, inside and out, for any sign that Measles had returned. Nothing. Nothing at all. They asked the neighbors on either side of Mrs. Caldwell if they had heard any meowing at night, which might mean the cat was still around, but the neighbors had heard nothing. And then they discovered that someone had written on their Missing Cat posters. What someone had written, in fact, right over their names and phone numbers, was DON'T HIRE THESE PET SITTERS THEY AREN'T ANY GOOD.

"Kimberly Evans and Ellen Ann!" Josie cried, tearing the poster down.

"Oh, I *hate* them!" said Sarah. "People will read this and *no* one will hire us! We need a miracle, Josie, and we need one quick!"

They checked the other cat notices. There was the same scribbled message on all of them. The girls took them down and walked back to Josie's.

They had just stepped through the door when the phone rang. Clyde, who was reading the sports page, walked across the room in his stocking feet to answer.

"Hello?" he said. And then there was a pause. "Greg Maloney!" he said in astonishment. "My gosh! The football player?" And then, after another pause, "You sure you got the right number?"

The whole family stared; Vernon and Mr. Wells from the sofa, Mother from her chair by the window. Josephine and Sarah were still standing in the doorway with their posters. And Clyde was saying over and over again, "I can't believe it's you!"

Josie's heart was in her mouth. She knew why the quarterback was calling. This was the miracle she had been hoping for. Just when Josie needed it most, Greg Maloney was coming through with the money!

Then Clyde turned toward her, holding out the telephone, a look of astonishment on his face. "Josie!" he said. "Greg Maloney wants to talk to you!"

"To *Josie?*" said Mother and Dad together. Josie heard Sarah swallow.

She went to the telephone. "Hello?" She wished now that she had asked for a hundred dollars. A quarterback who earned a million dollars a year wouldn't miss a hundred dollars one bit.

Greg Maloney's voice was cheerful. "I got your letter, Josephine," he said, "and I appreciated all the nice things you said about my football playing."

"I meant them too," said Josie earnestly. "You're the best quarterback that ever lived." Maybe he'd give her a hundred dollars after all! Two hundred, even!

"I don't have a game till tomorrow night, so I thought I'd catch up on some phone calls," Greg Maloney said. "Wanted to see how you're doing."

"Well, we've still got forty-one dollars and fifty cents yet to earn," Josie said. She had to be truthful. She couldn't say she needed more than she did.

"That's what I'm calling about. You know, Josie, I had to work part-time all through high school; my folks couldn't pay a cent toward my college tuition. And I'm glad now they didn't help me out. The things you do for yourself mean a whole lot more to you in the long run. So don't get discouraged; earning that money yourself may be the best thing that ever happened to you."

The corners of Josie's mouth sagged. Had she heard right? This couldn't be happening! Greg Maloney was the only miracle left. There was silence on the line, however, and she had to say something. "Maybe so," she said disappointedly. "Anyway, thanks for calling."

"Good luck, Josie," the quarterback said.

Josie slowly hung up the phone.

"What did he say?" everyone was asking at once. "What did he want? Why was he calling *you*?"

"Because I wrote him a letter to say what a good football player he was," Josie said softly.

"*You* wrote to Greg *Maloney*?" asked her father.

"What were you saying about forty-one dollars and fifty cents?" her mother wanted to know.

"Oh, I was just telling him about breaking the piano-bench leg," Josie said.

The family continued to stare.

"Boy, Josie, you're really weird," said Vernon. "You write to Greg Maloney, the world's best quarterback, and tell him about breaking a leg on a piano bench?"

"Just wait till I tell everyone about talking to Greg Maloney!" broke in Clyde. "Man, oh man! What a thrill!"

Josephine and Sarah dropped the posters in Josie's bedroom and escaped as fast as they could. Once they were outside, Josie felt tears stinging her eyes.

"I really thought he'd give us the money," she sniffled. "Somehow I thought he wouldn't miss it, him being a millionaire and all."

"Well, you tried, Josie," Sarah said comfortingly. "It's back to raking leaves, I guess."

The afternoon had turned colder. The wind was nippy, making their cheeks red as they raked. Every time another gust crossed the mountain, another rush of leaves came floating down. When they had a pile collected, they stuffed them quickly in a bag before the wind blew them all over the yard again.

And then, as though there hadn't been enough trouble for one day, Caroline Prescott came back from the movies and said, "Sarah, have you seen what's on the telephone poles now?"

Sarah and Josie stared. They had taken their own posters down, so they couldn't imagine.

"*What?*" asked Sarah.

Caroline's voice was sympathetic. "Go look," she said gently.

Josie and Sarah dropped their rakes and ran to the nearest corner. There on the telephone pole was a brand-new poster with pictures of Kimberly and Ellen Ann on it.

THE PET FINDERS, it said. CAT MISSING? DOG LOST? CALL KIMBERLY EVANS OR ELLEN ANN JACOBS. WE GET RESULTS! And it gave the girls' phone numbers.

Josie felt as though the breath had been knocked out of her. She closed her eyes a moment and leaned against the pole. This would be the end of the pet- and plant-sitting business. Mrs. Caldwell would come home to find her cat missing, hire Kimberly and Ellen Ann to find it, and when they did, as they probably would, she would hire *them* to care for Measles the next time she left town.

Word would get around that Kimberly and Ellen Ann were better sitters, and Josie and Sarah would be out of business. Once they were out of business, the Prescotts would be angry that the girls had not been able to pay back the sixty dollars. They might forbid Sarah to play with Josie anymore. Then Sarah would team up with Kimberly and Ellen Ann, and . . . She pressed her lips together to keep from bawling.

"You know what I think?" said Sarah angrily. "I think that Kimberly is hiding Measles just so she can pretend she found him when Mrs. Caldwell comes back."

"Do you really think she'd do that?" Josie asked miserably.

"I didn't *used* to think Kimberly would do things like that. Kimberly used to be my best friend! Now that you're my best friend, Josie, I see just what kind of girl she really is. We're never going to speak to Kimberly Evans again, not even if she grows up and marries and invites us to her wedding! Not even if she asks us to be *brides*maids!"

Somehow this didn't make Josephine feel better. Having Sarah all to herself wasn't quite as wonderful as it had seemed once when she was looking for a special friend. If having someone as "best friend" meant being enemies with the other girls, then it wasn't the way Josie had hoped it would be.

At dinner that night, Josephine was very quiet.

"Cat got your tongue?" her father asked, reaching for the stewed tomatoes.

"Ha!" said Vernon. "Somebody's got the *cat's* tongue. In fact, somebody's got the whole cat!"

"Vernon, hush!" Mother scolded. Then, turning to Josephine, she said, "What's wrong?"

There was no use keeping it a secret any longer. "We're in more trouble, Sarah and me," Josie said.

Mother stopped chewing. "What kind of trouble?"

"Kimberly and Ellen Ann have started a pet-finding business," Josie said, and told how they would probably be the ones to find Measles and drive Sarah and Josie out of business, and the girls would never earn enough to pay for the piano bench.

"I *declare*, Josephine Ruth!" said her mother. "Every day you and Sarah seem to have more troubles than you did before."

"It's not Sarah's fault," Josephine said, not liking the tone of her mother's voice.

"Well, I would think that at *some* point the Prescotts would see that you girls have really tried, and consider the debt paid," said Father. "It's not as though the Prescotts are so poor that they can't pay for having that piano bench repaired themselves."

"That's those Prescotts for you," said Clyde, smearing a big pat of margarine on his bread. "You think that Caroline Prescott would give me a smile or anything when I pass her in the hall? Think she'd look up and say hello or something when I walk by her table in the cafeteria? Won't even offer me the time of day."

"Now, wait a minute," said Mother. "When Mrs. Prescott called here about the piano bench, she was as kind as could be. They're not *that* snooty."

"Ha! You should have seen *Sarah* when she won second place in the costume contest," Vernon put in. "Strutting around like a peacock!"

"She was not!" said Josie, and suddenly she wasn't hungry anymore. She put down her fork and left the table. The way Clyde kept talking about Caroline and Vernon kept talking about Sarah, they'd slowly turn Mother and Dad against the Prescotts too. It was all a matter of time, and their families would be enemies.

At school the next day, she and Sarah cornered Kimberly Evans out by the fence on the playground, forgetting their pledge never to talk to her again.

"Okay, Kimberly," Sarah said. "You took Measles just so you could pretend to find him when Mrs. Caldwell comes home. Give him back."

Kimberly's eyes were brown as pennies, and when she looked surprised, as she did then, her eyes grew as big as chestnuts.

"You think *I've* got him?" she asked.

"Yes!"

"I *don't* have Measles. I *never* took anybody's cat!" said Kimberly. And then, looking from one girl to the other: "But if he's still missing, you can bet Ellen Ann and I will find him!"

Josephine felt cold inside. She believed her.

Chapter Nine

A Strange Surprise

That evening, Clyde had a new story to tell about Caroline Prescott. Every day now, it seemed, there was another story about just how uppity she was.

Josie's father had scarcely asked the blessing, and the family had barely reached for their forks before Clyde said, "You won't *believe* what cuckoo Caroline did *today*."

As soon as Clyde said that, Josephine lost her appetite.

"What?" Vernon said. Vernon loved Clyde's "Caroline stories."

"I was standing right behind her in the cafeteria, and when the woman at the steam table put gravy on her meat loaf, Caroline asked her to take it off."

"Did the woman do it?" Vernon asked.

"No. She said that's the way the meat loaf came, and that Caroline should have told her sooner."

"So what happened?" asked Vernon.

"Cuckoo Caroline didn't eat any meat loaf at all. I think she bought a Mars bar instead."

"For somebody who can't stand Caroline Prescott, you're paying an awful lot of attention to her," Father said to Clyde.

"Ugh. She's so awful you just can't help staring," Clyde told him.

Josephine clunked down her glass of milk. "Well, *I* don't think she's awful. *I* think Caroline is beautiful and nice and kind." She didn't really think all *that* about Caroline Prescott, but somebody had to defend her.

"Beautiful?" said Clyde. "Beautiful like a bat, maybe."

There was no use talking with Clyde.

The next day after school, when the girls had walked Jaws, they went over the entire neighborhood searching for Measles again. They checked every alley, and even looked in trash cans.

"As soon as Caroline comes home from school, she begins," said Sarah, peering in a garage as they passed. "It's always another 'clumsy Clyde' story. How Clyde tripped on a chair coming into class. How he dropped a carton of milk in the cafeteria. How he was walking backward down the hall and bumped into the principal."

"I don't think he's very clumsy," Josephine said.

"I don't either," said Sarah, "but Caroline says he's so dangerous somebody ought to put a fence around him."

Josie stopped walking, pulled a tissue out of her jeans pocket, and blew her nose. "You know what's going to happen, don't you? Things will get worse and worse until your family is enemies with my family and they'll finally tell us not to speak to each other anymore."

"Well, if they do, I won't listen," said Sarah.

"Me either," said Josie.

The girls turned up the collars of their jackets as they started through another alley.

"Maybe we could go into the snow-shoveling business when winter comes," Josie suggested finally.

"Somebody would probably steal our snow shovels," Sarah brooded.

"We could offer to haul away old Christmas trees after the holidays," said Josephine.

"Somebody would probably steal our sleds," said Sarah.

"Maybe we could go around collecting old bottles and aluminum cans," said Josephine. "We could put up posters saying 'Old cans? Old bottles? Call Josephine and Sarah.' "

"The posters would disappear or get marked up," said Sarah. She stopped and faced Josephine. "Do you really think that Kimberly stole Measles?"

For a moment Josie didn't answer. "No," she said finally. "But I'll bet she finds him and then we're out of business."

They said good-bye at the corner and each went

back to her own house. And as if Josie wasn't feeling bad enough, she found a postcard waiting for her. It was from Mrs. Caldwell, saying she'd probably be returning in a few days. Josie felt a stomachache coming on and went to bed.

Josephine and Sarah's worries got them into even more trouble the next day. Sarah was caught passing a note to Josephine when the class was supposed to be taking an arithmetic test, and the teacher told Sarah to stay after school. The note said, *Ellen Ann really looks guilty! I'll bet she's the one who's got Measles.* If Sarah had only waited to tell Josephine instead of writing her a note, she wouldn't have been in trouble.

Josephine sat on the wall outside the building, played a game of hopscotch by herself, and was still waiting when Sarah got out fifteen minutes later.

"You're always getting me in trouble," Sarah said grumpily, starting off down the sidewalk.

Josie stared after her. "Sarah, it was *you* who sent the note! I didn't ask you to."

"I know," Sarah said miserably, "but Mom is going to be angry. I never had to stay after school until I met you."

"Well, *I* never got into so much trouble until I met *you!*" Josie snapped back.

The girls walked a block without speaking. Then Josephine said suddenly, "See, Sarah? It's just like I said it would be. After awhile, even *we'll* be enemies."

Sarah stopped walking and looked at her. "Let's

say it together then, Josie: 'We're friends forever, no matter what.' "

"We're friends forever, no matter what," the two girls said.

And then they got a surprise, because as they passed the hedge next to Josephine's house, they saw Kimberly Evans standing on the Wellses' front porch. She was just reaching out to press the doorbell when she heard the girls coming. When Kimberly turned around, Josie saw that she had a cat in her arms.

"Measles!" Josephine and Sarah cried together.

The cat almost jumped out of Kimberly's arms when it heard their voices, and when Kimberly handed him over, Josephine could see that the cat was still sleek and fat and well cared for.

"Where did you find him?" Sarah asked.

Kimberly was coldly polite. "Old Mrs. Wheeler down the street had him. Mom found out when she went to visit her. I guess Mrs. Wheeler's always wanted a cat, and when Measles wandered up on her porch, she just took him in and kept him. Mom saw your poster about the missing cat, so she asked me to bring him back."

Josephine and Sarah studied her. "You could have waited until Mrs. Caldwell came home and returned the cat to her," Josie said.

"I *could* have, but I didn't. You don't have to like me if you don't want, but I'd never do something like that."

"Listen, Kimberly," Sarah said. "The reason we didn't let you in on our sitting business is because we have to make a lot of money to pay my mom for breaking a piano-bench leg. Once we earn enough to pay for that, we probably won't even keep the business going."

"Well, I don't care *what* you do," Kimberly said, "but Ellen Ann and I are going to keep our pet-finders business, and it looks like we're off to a good start, even though we *don't* get paid for this one." And she walked away.

"Whew!" said Sarah. "We got Measles back just in time, Josie. We've got to hurry!"

If Mrs. Caldwell came home that evening, there was just enough time to take Measles back before she got there. Josephine and Sarah walked over to her house, went inside with the cat, and locked the door after them. They put fresh food in Measles's dish, fresh water in his bowl, and fresh litter in his box. Measles seemed glad to be home, and went about from room to room, sniffing and purring.

After the girls had locked him securely inside, they went to the Garsons' to walk Jaws, and no sooner were they home again than the phone rang. It was Mrs. Caldwell.

"I just wanted you to know that I'm home, and it was *so* good to find my Measles safe and sound," she said. "He looks nice and healthy, and you girls must have taken wonderful care of him."

"He was missing for a while," Josie volunteered. "We can't accept any money for the days he was gone."

"Well, cats have a way of doing that, but the main thing is he's home again where he belongs," Mrs. Caldwell told her. "Come by later, dear, and we'll figure out what I owe you."

"Yes, ma'am!" Josie said, relieved.

Mrs. Wells invited Sarah to stay for dinner. Clyde didn't say anything bad about Caroline Prescott with Sarah there, and Vernon didn't say anything bad about Sarah, and after the girls had collected their pay from Mrs. Caldwell, Josie began to think that if they could ever get the piano bench paid for, and make up with Kimberly and Ellen Ann, life in Webster Springs might be pretty wonderful. After all, it might be nice to have *three* good friends instead of just one. *Three* other houses to spend the night in. *Four* girls roller-skating down the hill instead of only two. But Kimberly Evans was so angry at them that Josie wondered if she would even *want* to be friends.

The following evening, when the Wellses were eating dinner, Clyde began his Caroline Prescott stories again, but this one was a little different.

"You won't believe what I'm going to do Friday night," he said, his mouth half full of biscuit. "It'll be a real gas! I'm going to take Caroline Prescott to the movies."

Josie almost dropped her fork. So did Vernon.

"I thought you didn't like her," said Josie.

"I don't! I just want to see how conceited she really is."

"Seems to me you're going to a lot of trouble for a girl you can't stand," said his father.

Clyde gave a little laugh. "I just want to have some fun, that's all."

"Have you actually *asked* her?" Mother wanted to know. "Did she say yes?"

"Yeah, she'll go. Probably just wants to give me a hard time."

"Clyde, you behave yourself now," said his father.

"I'll be the perfect gentleman," said Josie's brother.

When Sarah came over later and the girls went to the Garsons' to walk Jaws, Josie said, "I can't believe that Clyde and Caroline are going out together."

"Me either," said Sarah. "Caroline says she's only going out with him to see how gross and clumsy he can be. She says he'll probably fall up the front steps just getting to the door, and stick french fries up his nose to be cute."

"Well, I hope they make each other sick," said Josie. "If they don't like each other, why don't they just go out with someone else?"

"I hope we never act like that when we're sixteen," said Sarah.

Walking Jaws had become the best part of each day for Josephine and Sarah. The Great Dane seemed to look forward to their coming, for as soon as they came up the sidewalk toward the house, he would yelp with delight, stand up on his hind legs by the front door, his stub of a tail wagging like crazy.

The only thing the girls had to look out for was cats and squirrels and other dogs. At the street corners, before crossing, when Josie and Sarah said "stop," Jaws stopped. When he took too long sniffing around fire hydrants and hedges, and the girls said "go!," Jaws went.

But if he saw anything at all on four legs, he took off like a speedboat. Josie had to hold on for dear life, Sarah holding on to her.

When they had returned Jaws to the Garsons' that evening, Josie said, "Why don't you stay overnight with me, Sarah? We've got to go over our money again and see how much we can pay your mother this week."

So Sarah brought her toothbrush and pajamas to Josie's, and they figured up how much they still owed on the piano bench, trying to decide what they would do for presents for their families when Christmas came, since they would still be in debt even then.

As they sat on Josie's bed, their backs against the wall, Sarah said, "Who's that talking?"

Josie listened. "It's Clyde, on the other side of the wall. He's probably on the phone."

"Well, I heard him say 'Caroline.' "

Josie crept to the door and looked out. The telephone cord was stretched across the floor and ran under the door of Clyde and Vernon's room. She and Sarah giggled.

Josephine went to the kitchen and came back with two drinking glasses. She showed Sarah how to hold the open end up to her ear, the other end against the wall. They grinned at each other as they listened.

"Well, I don't really care what movie we see either," Clyde was saying. ". . . I mean, if you don't want to go. . . . Of course I want to take you. I asked, didn't I? . . . I never said that about your hair! Who said I said that about your hair?"

Josie almost fell off the bed laughing. Then she stopped because her father was standing in the doorway. Josie slowly lowered the drinking glass in her hand. So did Sarah.

"Well, well, I see you've got thirsty ears," Josie's father said, coming into the room. "Shall I go fill the glasses for you? What would you like in your ear, Josie? Seven-Up? Coke okay for you, Sarah?"

Sarah's face turned pink, but Mr. Wells was laughing, and Josie and Sarah laughed too.

"No listening," said Josie's father, and he shut the door.

The next day, when Josie and Sarah set out to walk Jaws, the huge dog seemed especially happy to be outside.

He didn't walk, he pranced. He could barely contain himself at the street corners when the girls said "stop." He was off again before they said "go." But just as they started up the block, Jaws caught sight of a new cat.

BAND

The problem was that Jaws saw it before Josie and Sarah did. By the time Josie tried to wrap the leash twice around her hand, Jaws had started off like a shot, taking the leash with him. And at the far end of the long block was the busiest street in Webster Springs.

Josie screamed. Sarah shrieked. People saw the Great Dane coming and got out of the way fast. One man tried to step on the leash, but the dog was gone before he knew it. On Jaws went until someone, far down the sidewalk—*two* someones, in fact—lunged forward as Jaws went by, fell on the leash, and stopped him in his tracks.

Josie and Sarah ran up just as Kimberly and Ellen Ann got to their feet.

"Kimberly!" cried Sarah. "You stopped him!'

"*Thanks*!" Josie said. "He just got away. He saw a cat and was gone before we could catch him."

Jaws was still trying to get away, leaping up against the trunk of the tree where the cat had taken refuge, the cat's tail as thick as a hairbrush.

"I know," said Kimberly. "We've been trying to catch this stray to give to Mrs. Wheeler. She was so sad when we had to return Measles."

"We figured maybe a pet-finder could also look for a pet for someone who didn't have one," Ellen Ann told them.

What a great idea, Josie thought.

"He's really friendly, isn't he?" said Ellen Ann, petting Jaws.

"The Garsons call him 'Gentle Jaws,' " Sarah said.

Both Kimberly and Ellen Ann stroked the Great Dane. For a while all four of them stood there on the sidewalk, catching their breath and admiring Jaws.

"If he'd run out into the street, he'd have got hit," Kimberly said.

"I know," said Josie. "So far we've had really bad luck. We sure don't need anything happening to Jaws."

"Well, so far, all we've found is Measles, but Mrs. Caldwell never knew it was us who returned him," Kimberly said. "If we could just catch this stray cat for Mrs. Wheeler, maybe *we'd* be in business."

And then all four girls thought of it at once.

"Why don't . . . ?" Sarah began.

". . . all four of us . . ." said Kimberly.

"Go into business together," finished Josie and Ellen Ann. And then they laughed.

"Pets and Plants, Sitters and Finders," said Josie.

"Let's *do* it!" said Sarah. "We'll have to split the profits four ways, but with all of us working, we ought to bring in more customers."

"The first thing to do is get this cat," said Kimberly. "Any ideas?"

"I'm a pretty good climber," said Josie, tying Jaws's leash to the tree.

"Why don't you go up then, Josie, and hand the cat down to me," Kimberly suggested. "I'll climb up just behind you."

So Ellen Ann gave Josie a boost and up she went. The stray cat was on a branch just above her. As Josie got closer she could see that the cat was thin and scraggly.

"Here, kitty!" she called. The cat went higher, but only a little way. And when at last Josie put one hand around her, the cat remained still, allowing herself to be lifted, and even managed a purr when Josie placed her in the waiting arms of Kimberly.

"Mother said this cat's been hanging around the neighborhood for several weeks, meowing and wanting to be fed," Kimberly said when the girls were on the ground again. "Our first job, Ellen Ann! Mrs. Wheeler said she'd pay a dollar if we could find a cat to replace Measles."

"One dollar split four ways," said Ellen Ann.

"And we'll divide our dog-walking money today with you," said Sarah.

The next evening all four girls got together at Josie's and made new posters to put up on telephone poles around the neighborhood, with school photos of all four of them. Josie's father had brought home some old posters from the video store that said EXCITING! EXTRAORDINARY! WONDERFUL! about a film. Josie cut out these words and pasted them at the top of their own poster to describe their new "Pets and Plants, Sitters and Finders" business.

"Why didn't we think of this before?" Sarah wondered aloud. "It'll be a lot more exciting."

Clyde walked by the kitchen table where they were working.

"Hey! Expanding the business, I see!" he said.

Josie sniffed the air. Something smelled good. It smelled like her father's Old Spice cologne. She looked at her brother.

Clyde had on his good sport coat and a red tie. He looked as though he were going to church. Then she remembered. He was taking Sarah's sister to the movies. She told Kimberly and Ellen Ann about it.

"Have a good time,
With Car-o-line!"

she sang out, as Clyde took his father's car keys and went out the back door.

"Say something nice about her hair," Sarah called after him.

"And don't kiss her too hard," said Josie. The four girls burst into laughter.

The next day Clyde didn't have any Caroline stories to tell.

"How was your date with Cuckoo Caroline?" Vernon snickered at lunch as Josie and her brothers made themselves sandwiches.

"It went pretty well," Clyde said. "She's changed a lot."

Josephine went to the phone and called Sarah. "I

think Clyde had a good time on their date," she whispered.

"So did Caroline," Sarah told her. "I asked her this morning if Clyde fell up the steps getting to the front door, and she said he wasn't as clumsy as she'd thought, but she'd have to go out with him again to make sure."

Josie and Sarah laughed out loud.

Friends. That made all the difference in a new town. Clyde had just discovered it, but Josie had learned something more: one new friend was nice, but two were even better. And *three* new friends, *best* friends, were better still.